W9-BEA-919

Franklin's Baby Sister

To Cole and Rachel Shearer — P.B.
For my baby sister, Linda, with love — B.C.

Franklin is a trademark of Kids Can Press Ltd.

Text copyright © 2000 by P.B. Creations Inc.
Illustrations copyright © 2000 by Brenda Clark Illustrator Inc.

Interior illustrations prepared with the assistance of Shelley Southern.

Kids Can Press acknowledges the financial support of the Ontario Arts Council,
the Canada Council for the Arts and the Government of Canada, through the
BPIDP, for our publishing activity.

Kids Can Press Ltd.
29 Birch Avenue
Toronto, Ontario, Canada
M4V 1E2

Printed in Hong Kong by Wing King Tong Company Limited

CDN PA 00 0 9 8 7 6 5 4 3 2

Canadian Cataloguing in Publication Data

Bourgeois, Paulette
        Franklin's baby sister

ISBN 1-55074-794-0 (bound)   ISBN 1-55074-858-0 (pbk.)

I. Clark, Brenda. II. Title.

PS8553.O85477F724 2000   jC813'.54   C00-930336-7

PZ7.B68Fr 2000

Kids Can Press is a Nelvana company

Franklin's Baby Sister

Written by Paulette Bourgeois
Illustrated by Brenda Clark

Kids Can Press

FRANKLIN could count by twos and tie his shoes. He could name the days of the week, the months of the year and the four seasons. He liked to play ball in summer, collect leaves in fall and build snow turtles in winter. But Franklin loved spring most of all. And this spring promised to be very special.

Franklin's parents had exciting news. They were
going to have a baby in the spring.

Franklin jumped up and down. He had always
wanted to be a big brother. He had even practised
with Bear's little sister, Beatrice.

"I can make babies laugh, and I can burp them,
too," said Franklin.

"You will be a wonderful big brother," said
his mother.

Every day, Franklin asked his parents, "Is it spring yet?"

Franklin's mother would pat her tummy and say, "Not yet. But soon."

Franklin wasn't so sure. It was still cold outside, and there was snow on the ground. Spring seemed far away.

At school, Mr. Owl asked if anyone knew the signs of spring.

"The earth wakes up after a long sleep," said Badger.

"Plants start pushing through the ground," said Snail.

"Babies are born," said Franklin.

He looked out the window at the wintery sky and wished that spring would hurry up.

Franklin worried about the seed he'd planted for his spring project.

"It's in a warm, safe place, and it always has water," he told Mr. Owl. "But nothing is happening."

"Your plant is growing," said Mr. Owl. "You just can't see it yet. You'll have to wait."

Franklin sighed. He didn't like waiting.

At home, Franklin helped his parents get ready for the baby.

"It sure is taking a long time for this baby to get here," said Franklin.

Franklin's mother gave him a hug. "The baby is due in spring, and spring is just around the corner," she said.

"It is?" said Franklin, brightening.

Franklin went for a walk. He looked around every corner and called, "Hello, Spring? Are you there?"

But there was no answer.

Franklin banged on pots and clanged on pans. He rang bells and clashed cymbals.

Even with all the noise, the earth didn't wake up.

Franklin looked in his garden. None of the plants had pushed through the ground.

There was no sign of spring anywhere.

And that was a problem because the baby was supposed to arrive in the spring.

Franklin felt very sad. If spring didn't come, he would never be a big brother.

Franklin moped around the yard.

His father came out to see what was wrong.

"I don't think spring will ever come," said Franklin.

"Don't worry," said his father. "April showers bring May flowers."

Franklin got excited. He knew that April and May meant spring. And they were having a shower that weekend. His mother had said so.

On Sunday, Franklin put on his rain gear and got his umbrella.

"I'm ready for the shower," he said.

"We're not having that kind of shower," laughed his mother. "It's a *baby* shower."

Franklin looked confused.

His father smiled. "Our friends bring gifts for the baby."

Franklin wished their friends would bring spring instead.

During the shower, some special presents arrived from Great-Aunt Harriet.

There was a mobile for the baby, flowers for Franklin's mother and a kite for Franklin.

Franklin's mother sniffed the blossoms and said, "It looks like Aunt Harriet sent us spring."

"Whoopee!" said Franklin. "The baby will be born soon."

The next day at school, Franklin announced that spring had sprung.

"You're right," agreed Mr. Owl. "Look."

Franklin's plant had pushed its way into the light. It was little and green and absolutely wonderful.

Beaver

Frankl

When Franklin got home, his granny was there.

"Congratulations, Franklin," she said. "You are a big brother. Your little sister was born today."

Franklin danced around the house.

"May I see her now?" he asked.

"She's waiting for you at the hospital," said Granny. And off they went.

At the hospital, Franklin kissed his parents and smiled at the baby.

"What's her name?" asked Franklin.

"We haven't decided yet," answered his mother. "We need something special."

Franklin looked closely at his sister. "Why don't we name her after Great-Aunt Harriet? She's special, and the baby looks just like her."

Franklin's mother and father smiled. They agreed that Harriet was the perfect name.

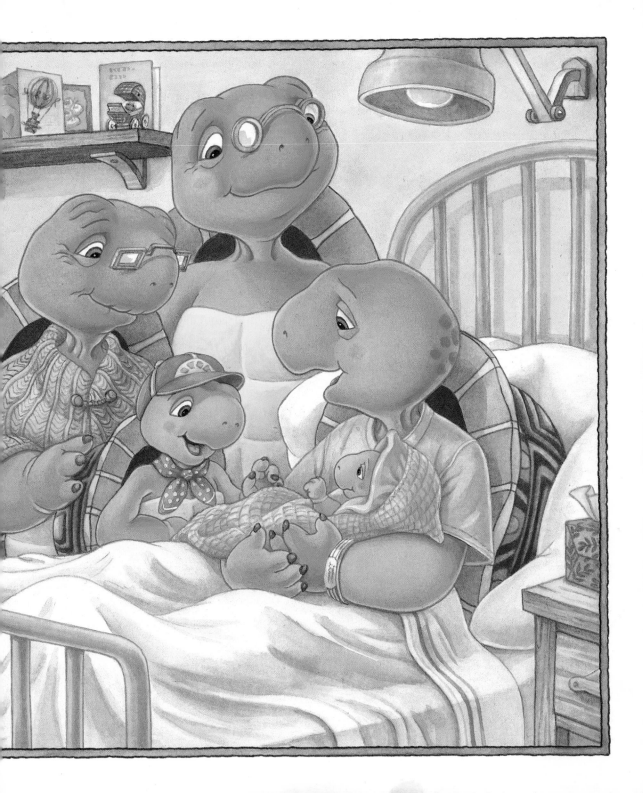

Franklin asked to hold his sister. He cradled her gently in his arms.

"Hello, Harriet," he said. "I'm your big brother, Franklin, and I've been waiting for you."